The Cinnamon Lake-Ness Monster Mystery

Dandi Daley Mackall
Illustrated by Kay Salem

D1417125

CPH
SAINT LOUIS

To my buddies Tess, Nancy, and Laurie—
the best writing group
God could have given me.
Thanks.

Copyright © 1998 Dandi Daley Mackall
Published by Concordia Publishing House
3558 S. Jefferson Avenue, St. Louis, MO 63118-3968
Manufactured in the United States of America

Library of Congress Cataloging-in-Publication Data

Mackall, Dandi Daley.
   The Cinnamon Lake-Ness Monster Mystery / Dandi Daley Mackall.
illustrated by Kay Salem.
      p.   cm. -- (Cinnamon Lake mysteries ; 7)
   Summary: When Moly and her friends investigate the appearance of a
monster in Cinnamon Lake, they discover that true courage comes from
trusting in Christ.
   ISBN 0-570-05336-6
   [1. Monsters--Fiction.   2. Christian life--Fiction.   3. Mystery and
detective stories.] I. Title. II. Series.
PZ7.M1905k   1998
[Fic]--dc21   97-44230
                                                                      AC

 2 3 4 5 6 7 8 9 10   07 06 05 04 03 02 01 00 99 98

Cinnamon Lake Mysteries

I'm not sure how we got famous
as the Cinnamon Lake Mystery Club.
I mean, the Cinnamon Lake part
is easy. That's where we live.
The mystery part is more ...
mysterious.

Contents

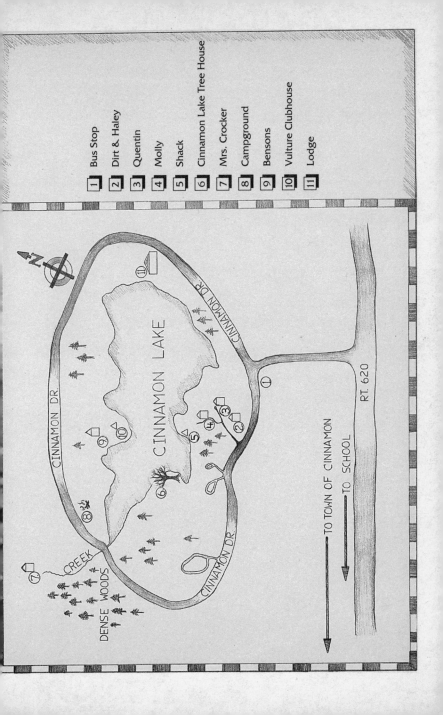

1	Bus Stop
2	Dirt & Haley
3	Quentin
4	Molly
5	Shack
6	Cinnamon Lake Tree House
7	Mrs. Crocker
8	Campground
9	Bensons
10	Vulture Clubhouse
11	Lodge

There's a Monster in My Lake!

"Ah-ee-eeee!"

The scream pierced the darkness. It reached all the way up to the top branch of the Cinnamon Lake tree house and made me shiver.

"What was that?" I asked.

"Molly," Dirt scolded from her branch just below mine, "don't you know Haley's scream by now?"

Haley's sister Dirt is two years younger than Haley and me. But she's the toughest first grader in the world. She stood up on her branch and balanced. Our Cinnamon Lake tree house was still all tree, no house. But on a clear summer night like this one, I didn't care.

I looked past Dirt to the lake. Pitch black night lay between our tree and the lake. Over Cinnamon Lake the moon lit up the far shore. I peered across the waters, but I couldn't see Haley.

"I would have to say that the scream is amplified," said Quentin in his scientific voice. "Volume increases as a result of travel across the lake."

Quentin and his little cousin Solomon sat side by side on the branch below Dirt's. Solomon had been visiting for only a week. And already Quentin talked about nothing but shipping him back to Chicago.

"Will you please move over, Solomon?" Quentin said. "Take Sunny's branch. She's in Hawaii, where I wouldn't mind resting myself—as long as you did not tag along there as well."

Solomon did as he was told and moved to Sunny's branch. "I do not believe you would find the Islands agreeable to your sensitive skin, Quentin," said Solomon. "Those harmful ultraviolet rays shine more directly there."

Solomon looked like a little Quentin. Glasses, a little pudgy, skin the color of chocolate milk. He even talked like Quentin. Just as scientific. I couldn't understand him half the time.

The scream came again, chilling my spine. "Should we go see what scared Haley?" I asked.

"That's her cockroach scream," Dirt said. "She yells like that when she sees anything bigger than an ant. Like cockroaches. We've got 'em in the basement."

"A bit of boric acid should take care of your cockroach problem," said Solomon. "You see, cockroaches cannot burp. When a cockroach eats the acid, the mixture bubbles in his stomach. The bubbles have nowhere to go. Therefore, the cockroach explodes from the inside out."

"Far out!" Dirt said. She let out a deep burp herself. "There's hope for you yet, Sol."

"Thank you, Roseanna," he said.

"You call me that again," Dirt said, "and I'll smash you!"

Dirt got her name because she's going to be an archaeologist. That's somebody who digs in the dirt. She loves dirt. Solomon may have been a year older than Dirt, but I had no doubt Dirt could smash him like a tomato.

"*Ayee!*" The scream came again, louder than ever.

"That's it," I said. "We have to go see what's wrong. What if the Vultures captured Haley?"

"Vultures?" Solomon repeated. "Vultures prefer dead animals."

"Not those vultures," Quentin said, moaning. "The club, Vultures. I've told you about them a million times!"

"I do believe you are exaggerating, Cousin," Solomon said. "A million times?"

I stepped in to keep the peace. "You know Sam Benson, Solomon," I explained. "He's in the Vultures' Club, and so is his big brother, Ben, the fifth grader. And the worst one, the leader, is—" Then I remembered. Marty, the leader of the Vultures, was Solomon's other cousin. Quentin and Marty are so different, I sometimes forget they're related. I finished my sentence. "—Marty, your cousin."

"I do recall mention of Martin's group," Solomon said.

"Listen up, Solly," Dirt said. "See that pad on the other side of the lake? Vultures. Get it? Bad guys."

She pointed across the lake. The metal roof of the Vulture clubhouse sparkled in the distance. The Vultures have a real clubhouse, with walls and everything. They call themselves Vultures because they love to destroy—mainly they destroy us.

The scream came so loud, it could have been in the tree with us. I heard a scuffling in the bushes. Branches cracked.

"Come on!" I said. "As president of the Cinnamon Lakers, I order everybody out."

"I'll go first!" Solomon said. He scooted to the edge of his branch and dropped to the ground.

"Ow!" came a yell—not Solomon's. "No fair!"

"Haley?" I asked.

"I've got somebody!" Solomon yelled. "I've got them now!"

"Stop it!" cried Haley. "Get him off me!"

I jumped down the other way and pulled Solomon off Haley. "Solomon," I said, "it's Haley."

He backed away, breathing hard.

"Keep that little twit off me!" Haley whined. "What's he doing here anyway?" Haley got to her feet. "Out of my way!" She shoved Solomon and me and started climbing the tree.

"Haley," I said, "the Cinnamon Lake meeting is over."

"Not for me, it's not," she said. "I'm not coming down there." Haley's hair, usually perfect, stuck out in all directions. Her skirt hung crooked, and her blouse bunched out of the waist.

"What's going on, Haley?" I asked, another shiver traveling along my spine. "What's the matter with you?"

"I'll tell you what's the matter with me," she said. "I just saw a monster in Cinnamon Lake!"

2

Moonlight Monsters

"A monster ... in Cinnamon Lake?" Quentin said. "Actually, Haley, this is a flight of fantasy unworthy even of you. Solomon, take note of what can happen when one fails to use the gray cells one has been given—few though they be."

Quentin calls thinking "using his gray cells." Haley didn't look as if she had a clue what Quentin was saying. But she knew it was an insult.

"Oh yeah?" Haley said. "Well, I saw a monster in Cinnamon Lake. I saw it as clear as day."

"I will take this nonsense as my cue to depart," Quentin said. "I have more important business—*real* business—to do in my laboratory. That is ..." he frowned at his little

13

cousin, "… if certain young people have not ruined any more of my experiments."

Quentin walked away. Solomon hurried after him. But Quentin turned on him. "Absolutely not, Solomon," he said. "I do not need a little pest for a shadow."

Quentin took one trail, and Solomon turned off onto another.

"Now, Haley," I said, trying my best to calm her down. "Tell us what you saw. You know there's no such thing as monsters."

"All right," Haley said. "I was crossing by the lake. Even though I hate these night meetings."

"I know, Haley," I said. "Go on."

"Well," she continued, "as I got close to the lake, I heard an unusual sound, like a cat crying."

"Probably was a cat crying," Dirt said.

"It was not!" Haley said.

"Was too," Dirt said.

"Was not!"

"Stop!" I pleaded. "Haley, go ahead."

"Well, I looked in the water and saw ripples. I heard a big splash. Then I saw this huge, ugly orange head glaring at me from the water!"

14

"That's easy," Dirt said. "Your reflection."

Haley ignored her. "It was awful—with huge, jagged teeth and hollow eyes! I screamed, but you were all too scared to come and save me."

"Scared?" Dirt said. She slapped me on the shoulder. "Come on, Molly. Let's meet the monster."

"Wait!" I said. I couldn't help it. I knew Haley's imagination. And I knew there were no such things as monsters. Still, the idea of going down to check it out made my blood run cold. "Maybe we should wait for Quentin," I suggested. "And daylight? Daylight's good."

Dirt cocked her head to one side and narrowed her eyes at me. "Come on, Molly. Don't tell me you're scared."

"I'm not scared," I lied. I tried to stare back at Dirt. She's hard to say no to. "Okay," I said at last. "But I can't stay very long. Mom will get worried."

Dirt took off through the woods. I trotted after her.

"Wait!" squealed Haley. "You can't just leave me here." She climbed cautiously down the tree.

"Come on, Haley," I called.

By the time Haley and I reached the lake, Dirt was already poking around in the mud with a big stick. "Come on, Monster," she called. "Here, Monster, Monster, Monster."

"It's not funny!" Haley whined, hiding behind me. "You're too close to the shore. It was out farther."

Dirt waded into Cinnamon Lake. She was barefoot, as always. She kept walking until the water was up to her knees. "Now what?" she said. "Molly, are you coming or what?"

"I've got my shoes on," I said.

"So?" Dirt said. "Take them off."

I didn't want to, but I kicked off my thongs. I waded out to Dirt. Seaweed felt slimy against my ankles. We were in the part of the lake that Bingo Bob, the caretaker, didn't like us to swim in.

"Let's get out of here, Dirt," I said. "I don't see anything."

I turned back toward the shore. All of a sudden, something broke the surface of the water with a splash. A roar came from behind me. I screamed and tried to run for the shore. But the water pushed against my knees and kept me from running.

"Help!" I screamed. "Dirt, run!" I moved closer to the shore, pushing my legs forward with all my might.

Behind me came the growl again.

I screamed and leaned in toward the shore. Something grabbed my ankle. I fell face forward into the mud and slime. "Let me go!" I screamed. "Let me—"

But I stopped cold. Instead of the growl, I heard ... laughter.

Seaweed was wrapped around my ankle. I pulled it free and got to my feet, dripping wet. I turned back to see Sam Benson.

"Oooh, monster!" he said, waving a big pumpkin on a stick. He laughed so hard, he choked and coughed.

"Very funny, Sam Benson," I said. "Look what you've done to my clothes!" I wiped slime off my face.

Dirt stood right where I'd left her, her hands on her hips. "You *are* a monster, Sam," Dirt said calmly.

"Well, he's not *my* monster," Haley whined from the shore.

"You can say that again," Sam said.

Ben Benson and Marty jumped up from behind a bush. "Roar!" they said, making the same sound I'd heard earlier. Then they burst out laughing. Ben and Marty are in fifth grade, but they're bigger than some high school kids. They walked toward us, the moonlight shining off Ben Benson's dark hair.

"I'm going home," I said, shaking the lake out of my ears.

Sam, still cackling, followed me toward the shore. Dirt passed us easily.

Suddenly a roar came from behind us, ten times as loud as Marty's and Ben's roars put together.

"What was that?" Sam asked, not laughing now.

"That wasn't us, was it, Marty?" Ben asked.

"No, it wasn't us, dummy," Marty said. "So what—"

Behind Ben and Marty, the water seemed to swell right before our eyes. Out of the water burst an enormous figure with long arms and a horrible, long neck!

Haley, Sam, Dirt, and I stared, wide-eyed and openmouthed, at the water behind Ben and Marty. I pointed to warn them. But no words came out.

"Right," Marty said. "Like we're going to fall for that old trick."

"Th-th-there!" Sam said, pointing behind them. The monster's body, covered with branches, rose from the water, as if rearing in the moonlight.

Slowly, Ben and Marty turned around toward the creature. It must have been only 20 feet from where they stood on the shore.

"Ah-h-h-h-h!" Their screams made Haley's sound like a whisper.

We turned our backs on Cinnamon Lake and ran as fast as we could through the woods, bumping into one another. We had barely escaped from the Cinnamon Lake Monster!

3

Screams & Schemes & Monster Dreams

I struggled to free myself. The monster closed in on me. I kicked with all my might. But the monster's arms folded around my legs. I tried to push him away. But the creature wrapped himself tightly around me. I could barely move.

I cried out. "Help! Let me go!"

The monster's fingers pressed on my shoulder, shaking me ...

"Mowry okey dokey?" Chuckie, my little brother, shook my shoulder again. "Mowry wake?"

I opened my eyes, never more thankful to be in my own bed. My flowered blanket had wrapped itself around me like a sleeping bag.

21

Chuckie squinted down at me. I stared up into his chocolaty face. "I'm okey dokey, Chuckie," I said, working myself free from the blanket. It was the first nightmare I could remember since the time I tried out for the first-grade play.

"How'd you get chocolate faced already, Chuckie?" I asked. Chuckie had probably started out pretty clean. Now, his cowboy pajamas had a red stain on one side and something sticky green in the middle.

He grinned. His teeth looked purple.

"You must have slept soundly," Dad said when I came down for breakfast.

"Why are you here?" I asked. Dad works at an advertising agency in the city. He has to drive an hour to get there. So he's usually the first one out of the house.

"And good morning to you too," he said.

I kissed him good morning. "Morning, Dad."

"I have to give a presentation to a client in Martinville," he said. "How does this sound, Molly? Chuckie, you sit down too."

Chuckie scooched on my lap. Dad stood up and acted like he was pointing to an invisible board. "Dental glue is for you! Put more *bite* in your bite." Dad sat down. "So, what do you think? It's a slogan for the false teeth people."

"We love it, Dad," I said. although I didn't think it was one of Dad's best slogans. He's made up millions of slogans for everything from flashlights to alligators. I held Chuckie's hands and started him clapping.

"Dad," I said, feeling my way now. "Do you believe in monsters?"

Dad was throwing papers into his briefcase. "Monsters? Sure. Did you ever meet my boss?"

"Not people monsters. Monster monsters."

"No monsters!" Chuckie said. He squirmed off my lap and ran out of the kitchen.

"I'm with Chuckie," Dad said. "No monsters." He kissed me on top of the head. "Got to go, Molly."

After gobbling down a bowl of cereal, I gave Dirt a call. I asked her to meet me at Quentin's. What I felt like doing was staying in bed with the covers pulled over my head. But then I was in danger of falling asleep, and the nightmare might come back. I couldn't hide out at home for the rest of my life. Something had to be done about the Cinnamon Lake monster. Only I didn't want to be the one to go up against it.

Dirt was sitting cross-legged in Quentin's driveway when I got there. "They're in there," she said, pointing to the basement where Quentin has his laboratory.

Dirt banged on the door. Voices rose up the stairway.

"I've told you to stay away from my air compressor!" Quentin screamed. I'd never heard him so mad. "Now do you understand why?"

"I *am* seeing to its repair, Cousin," Solomon said. "You should have it back by—"

But Quentin didn't let him finish. "That is not the point! You have no respect for my scientific work. I should banish you from my laboratory!" Quentin shouted.

"But I have my own experiments to conduct," Solomon said.

"You? Ha!" said Quentin.

Dirt knocked again, so loudly the door might have caved in.

I heard footsteps on the stairs. Then the door opened, and Solomon stood in the entrance. "Yes?" he said.

"Let us in," Dirt said. She pushed the door, smashing Solomon behind it.

I followed Dirt down the stairs. "Quentin?" I called.

"Down here," he said. He stood over a table of glass tubes. They hung from a small wooden stand. Below them was some kind of weird machine. It looked like a cross between an electric razor and a drill.

Solomon passed quietly to a smaller table covered with screws and tools and wires and wheels.

"Quentin," I said, "Dirt and I need to talk to you."

"Mmmm," he said. He bent down and opened a drawer below the table. Then he opened and slammed more drawers, looking for something he couldn't find. "Solomon, did you take my tape player?" he asked.

"Quentin," I said louder, "I need you to pay attention."

Dirt surprised Quentin from behind and pushed a metal folding chair behind him. Quentin's knees buckled and he plopped down in the chair. "We saw the monster," Dirt said.

"Of course you did," Quentin said, pushing his glasses up on his nose.

"Dirt's not kidding," I said. Then I told him, play-by-play, all we saw the night before. "So you see, Quentin, it couldn't be the Vultures. They were more scared than I was. There really is a Cinnamon Lake monster!"

"Lake-Ness monster, perhaps?" Solomon said.

"A what?" I asked Solomon, who had sneaked into the conversation.

"A play on words. From the Loch Ness monster," he explained. "In 1933, an elderly couple claimed they saw a dinosaur-like monster in Loch Ness."

"That's a lake in Scotland," Quentin explained.

"Yes," Solomon continued. "Since that time, there have been well over 3,000 additional sightings."

"How would that Lake-Ness thing get to Cinnamon?" Dirt asked.

"It could not. And it has not," Quentin said. "It is not scientific." He stood up. "And I have real work to do."

Dirt put her hand on Quentin's shoulder and forced him back into the chair. "Use your science and get that thing out of our lake," she said.

Quentin folded his arms and sighed. "Foolishness."

"Come on, Quentin," I begged. "I wouldn't have believed it either if I hadn't seen the thing with my own two eyes. All I'm asking is that you see for yourself. And if you see it, you'll know what we have to do to get rid of it."

Quentin scowled. "Monsters. Unscientific fancies."

"Molly," Solomon said, "perhaps there is a logical explanation for what you saw. In 1938, off the coast of Africa, fishermen caught a gigantic fish. As it turned out, this fish, the coelacanth, had been thought to be extinct since prehistoric days."

"See, Quentin," I tried. "Maybe it will end up a great scientific discovery."

I could tell I'd scored a point when Quentin's eyebrows arched above the rim of his glasses.

"I do not believe you will succeed in involving my cousin in this enterprise,"

Solomon said. "Are you not aware of Quentin's fear of water?"

"I am *not* afraid of water!" Quentin protested. "I merely have the intelligence to understand its properties. And I know the amoeba count in a lake such as ours. A lack of desire to splash about in dark and dank waters should not be misinterpreted as fear."

I knew Quentin didn't swim. I'd suspected his fear of water for years. "You don't have to swim with it, Quentin," I said.

Quentin closed his eyes, and I could almost hear his gray cells whirring. Finally, he said, "If for no other reason than to end this nonsense so I may return to my experiments, I shall take on this ... creature."

"Great!" Solomon said. "What do we do, Quentin?"

"*We* do not do anything," Quentin said. "*I* shall conduct a simple experiment an hour after darkness this evening."

"What can I do to help?" I asked.

"Peanut butter cookies," Quentin said simply.

4

The Disappearance of Quentin

I hid from the monster, trying not to breathe. It had already eaten Quentin and Solomon and who knew how many other Cinnamon Lake kids. I wanted to save them. But fear kept me glued to my spot behind the eerie tree. The monster was so close, I could smell its peanut butter breath.

I held my breath. At least the horrible monster didn't know I was there. Didn't know me.

"MOLLY!" it called.

Terrified that the monster actually knew me by name, I tried to run. But it was as if it held me frozen, hypnotized. I couldn't move. I heard the creature moving closer.

"MOLLY!" *it called again, as through a* *thick fog.*

"Molly! Molly!"

I opened my eyes. The monster was gone. But somebody was still calling my name. "Molly!"

I rubbed my eyes and got out of bed. The shout was coming from outside my window. I stumbled in the darkness, feeling my way to the window. The sun was just starting to rise.

Solomon appeared in a shadow below my window. He waved for me to come down.

I sighed and stretched. Then things came back to me. Quentin. His experiment. Dirt and I had made a couple dozen peanut butter cookies. We ran them to Quentin's after dinner. Dirt tried to talk Quentin into letting her go along as backup. But he said he had to conduct his monster experiment on his own. I knew Quentin still didn't believe us. And I didn't care much. I was just glad he didn't want us to go along with him to hunt the monster. The thought of going down to the lake again terrified me.

Haley and Dirt had come home with me to play Monopoly. Dirt quit when we wouldn't let her buy the jail. Haley whined every time she landed on my property. I was so tired from nightmares, I fell asleep and my head plopped down right on Boardwalk and Park Place.

I pulled on my swimsuit, shorts, T-shirt, and thongs and raced outside. It was so early, not even Chuckie was up.

Solomon was waiting for me on the doorstep. "You have to come right now," he said. "I do not know what to do. I have tried reason and logic and—"

"Slow down, Solomon," I said. "I'm barely awake. Start over."

"You do not suppose, do you, that my cousin attempted to enter Cinnamon Lake by himself? I do not believe he can swim." Solomon paced Mom's flower garden, his hands clenched behind his back.

"I think Quentin *can* swim," I said. "He just hates to. The water scares him for some reason."

"Be that as it may," said Solomon, fidgeting with his glasses just like his cousin, "Quentin has disappeared."

"What are you talking about?" I asked. For a second I thought I might still be in the middle of one of my nightmares.

"My cousin! He has not been home all night. I looked in his room this morning to ask how he had fared with the monster. He was gone. Missing. Vanished."

Solomon and I ran as fast as we could to the shore of Cinnamon Lake. The kid surprised me. He was pretty fast for a scientist. But I still got there first.

"Quentin!" I yelled.

Only the caw of a crow and flapping of wings answered.

"Quentin! Where are you?"

Solomon, puffing, out of breath, slipped down the bank. He caught himself and joined me. "Did you find him?" he asked.

I shook my head and felt a lump in my throat. I had as good as sent Quentin on this dangerous mission. If anything happened to him ... "Look for footprints!" I yelled to Solomon.

Tiny, clawed footprints made light tracks in the muddy bank. Plover. Those little, long-legged birds that look like small sandpipers. I recognized raccoon tracks that looked like baby handprints. But no Quentin.

Then Solomon cried out in his hoarse voice, "Molly! Could these be footprints?" He was crouched under a big willow tree, several yards from where Sam, Dirt, and I had seen the monster.

I ran to see what Solomon had found. In the dirt were deep footprints. Not bare feet or sandals or thongs, like most people wear by the lake. Not fishing boots either. The heel print was smooth and the sole deep. Somebody Quentin's size had made these prints. With shoes like Quentin's. *Quentin.*

"Solomon," I said, "I think these are your cousin's footprints. Stay out of the way. I'll follow them."

A clear set of prints led down to the water and back out. But the steps leaving Cinnamon Lake looked different. They zigzagged—first one way, then the other. Some of the prints were smudged. Others had only half a shoe print, as if Quentin had toppled, ready to fall over.

"Molly?" Solomon said, behind me. "What's wrong with these prints? Why was Quentin walking funny?"

I ignored Solomon. I couldn't think of anything but Quentin. Why had I made him look for the monster? Why didn't I leave everything alone? I'd been too scared to come with him. But that hadn't stopped me from sending him.

The prints disappeared into the woods, and I lost the trail. My heart was thumping so hard. I called back to Solomon, "Try to pick up the footprints somewhere else." But I had a sick feeling in my stomach. We weren't going to find any more prints.

"Molly, look!" Solomon cried out.

I turned and ran, hoping against hope for more tracks. Solomon was pointing at the dry dirt a few feet from the lake.

"I don't see any prints," I said.

"Not prints. But what are those?" he asked.

I got down on my knees to examine the specks Solomon pointed to. "Crumbs," I said. I shooed away a blue jay pecking at some of the crumbs. Gently, I picked up several crumbs and set them in the palm of my hand. Then I smelled. "Peanut butter," I whispered.

"Peanut butter?" Solomon repeated it so loud his voice cracked. "Then Quentin's gone—"

"The monster must have eaten the peanut butter cookies," I said. A picture flashed through my mind. The horrible creature chomping peanut butter cookies, looking around for more. "But that wasn't enough," I said, thinking aloud. "The monster was still hungry. He saw Quentin standing there and—"

"Will you two be quiet?"

The gruff voice behind us shook me from my little gray cells to my thongs. "Ah-h-hhhh!" I screamed, louder than Haley when she first saw the monster.

I spun around to see none other than Bingo Bob. Bingo Bob is the caretaker of Cinnamon Lake. He's big and reminds me of a mountain man. "It's only you," I said. All my muscles seemed to melt with the fright, leaving me like limp lettuce. I stumbled backward, bumping into Solomon and knocking his glasses off.

"Great," said Bingo Bob. "Now *all* the fish are scared off. I came over to ask you to keep your voices down. I've got fish lines in the lake." Bingo Bob caught more fish out of Cinnamon Lake than everybody else put together. He knew everything about fishing, including that you're not supposed to yell around the fish.

"Sorry, Mr. Bingo," I said. "But have you seen Quentin? We've lost him."

"If I had seen him, I'd have shooed him away too. I've asked you not to mess around down here. This end of the lake is where the bass hide." He pointed to the tall reeds that grew thickest on this side of the lake. "They like that there tall grass. You have the whole rest of the lake. Leave the bass in peace."

"But Quentin's disappeared," I explained. I wanted to tell somebody, make some grown-up believe us about the Lake-Ness monster. "I know you won't believe us, but we think there's a monster in Cinnamon Lake. Solomon calls it the Cinnamon Lake-Ness monster."

"Cinnamon Lake-Ness monster?" Bingo Bob said, without a trace of smile on his rough face. "I'm the right one to come to," he said. "I can help."

"You can?" I said. I brushed the dirt off my shorts. "You believe us?"

"Sure. I collect monsters. You kids go away. I'll fish and catch your monster. Now shoo."

So he didn't believe us either. I couldn't blame him.

"But Quentin actually has disappeared, Mr. Bingo," Solomon said.

Bingo Bob growled the words, "Smart boy, that Quentin. You two ought to try that disappearing act yourselves. I gotta get back to my fishing rods." He turned to go.

Solomon started to follow him, but I put out a hand to stop him. "It's no use," I said. "We'll have to get Dirt and Haley and start a search party."

Solomon and I checked the ground one more time. Blue jays and orioles had pecked up most of the cookie crumbs. I didn't see any new footprints.

From somewhere down the shore, a loud cry reached us. "What on earth?!" It sounded like Bingo Bob.

Solomon and I stared at each other. "Quentin!" I said.

We took off running down to Bingo Bob. He was standing on the shore, not far from the weeds. His pole was bent into an arch as he leaned back and pulled against something in the water.

"It's the biggest fish I've caught in here," said Bingo Bob. He's one of the biggest people I've ever known. But he had met his match. His hip-wader boots dug into the mud while he tugged on the line.

"It's the monster!" I said, trembling. I hid behind Bingo Bob. "Let it go!"

"Are you kidding?" he said. He turned his reel. It creaked and groaned. Then something huge popped out of the water. Bingo Bob fell backward on me. Something sailed over our heads and landed with a thud behind us.

I screamed. Solomon screamed. Bingo Bob scurried to his feet to see what he had caught. He bent into the bushes behind us and reached down. I held my breath.

Bingo Bob stomped out of the bushes. He raised his hook in the air. Dangling from his line were bones!

5

Diving for Dirt

I stared at the bleached white bones dangling from Bingo Bob's fishing pole. End to end, they stood taller than Solomon and me put together. Tears streamed down my cheeks. "Quentin," I said, sobbing.

Bingo Bob looked at me like I was crazy. "Not them bones," he said. He pulled his hook out of the top bone. The bones formed part of a skeleton of some kind. "Deer."

"Yes?" I said, touched that Bingo Bob would call me *dear.*

"Deer," he repeated. "Deer bones."

Solomon ran up to examine them. "It's not Quentin?" he said. "I mean, of course it's not Quentin. Had he drowned, his bones would not look like this. But how would deer bones get in the lake?"

"Maybe the monster eats deer?" I suggested.

"Deer bones all over back in the forest," Bingo Bob said. He threw the bones deep into the woods. "Can't say how they got in the lake. I'm going home."

Solomon and I walked back to Quentin's in silence. I wanted to see if I could pick up any clues from Quentin's room. And we could call Dirt and Haley for the search. I hoped Quentin's mother was at work. I didn't know how we'd break the news to her.

We climbed the hill to take the shortcut. At the top of the hill, I saw Dirt coming toward us.

"Hey, what's the racket? You guys are scaring my bats," she said.

"Bats?" Solomon asked.

I explained that Dirt takes care of baby bats in the woods.

"So," Dirt demanded, "what's happening, man?"

I told Dirt about Quentin and the bones and Bingo Bob.

Dirt didn't say anything, but she led the way to Quentin's house.

Solomon went in the house first. On the kitchen counter was a note. Solomon read it aloud. "Quentin, I'm letting you sleep in this morning. Do clean up that basement, son. Granny Mae's coming over. And please be nice to Solomon."

"She doesn't even know Quentin's missing," I said. "Let's look for clues in his room."

Quentin's room didn't look like any kid's room I'd ever seen. One wall was covered with shelves of books. On the other wall, rows of bottles and boxes lined board shelves. Instead of pictures on the wall, Quentin had tacked up weird things. His first magnifying glass. A burned piece of cardboard from his first explosion. On his desk was a model of the brain. It made me want to cry to think of never seeing Quentin again.

"What do you think's happened to Quentin?" I asked.

Above Quentin's bed hung a poster of Albert Einstein. Dirt dived on to the bed. "Dunno," she said in midair. She landed on the pile of covers with a *plop.*

From under those covers came a groan.

Dirt felt the covers under her. "Found him," she said, not budging.

Quentin's wiry, black hair poked out from the covers.

Solomon and I ran over and hugged Quentin's head.

"Hey!" he said, his voice gravely. His eyes without his glasses looked like little slits. "Get off!"

"We thought you were dead!" I said, talking fast. "And then Bingo Bob didn't believe us about the monster and went fishing. And he caught your bones. Only they weren't your bones after all. Deer. So we came here to look. And you weren't here. Only you *were* here."

Quentin groaned and went back under his covers, pulling them over his head. Dirt slid to the floor with a *thud.*

After a while, Quentin gave up. He sat up in bed and pulled on his glasses. He was wearing cowboy pajamas just like Chuckie's. I tried not to smile.

"So, tell us, Quentin!" I urged. "Did you see the monster? Did it eat the cookies?"

"No monster," he said. "I must admit, however, there was unusual lake movement."

"See?" I said. "That was it!"

"I did not see a monster, Molly," Quentin said. "Anyway, unfortunately, I did not get an opportunity to investigate further."

"How come?" Dirt asked.

Quentin squirmed and stared at his pillow. "Those peanut butter cookies interfered," he said finally.

"Why?" I asked. "Did something eat them?"

"In a way," Quentin said. "Oh, all right. I ate them."

"All of 'em?" Dirt asked.

"It was a long wait," Quentin said, defending himself. "I kept eating. Before long, the cookies were gone. And I began to feel poorly. My stomach became overstimulated. I had to dash for the woods and regurgitate."

"Vomit," Solomon explained, when he saw Dirt's and my confusion. "That explains the wobbly footprints from the lake to the woods."

"You puked? Hurled?" Dirt asked. "On peanut butter?"

"Dirt," Quentin said, looking a little yellow, "please do not discuss that substance in my presence."

"Quentin?" The call floating up from the kitchen had to be Granny Mae's. "Come on, Grandson," she said. "None of your mother's good-for-you cereals this morning. I've brought your favorite. Peanut Butter Crunch!"

Dirt and I said hi to Granny Mae. If it hadn't been for Dirt, I would have stayed right there with Granny Mae, safe. I didn't want anything to do with that monster. But Dirt tugged until I had to leave. Quentin refused to go with us. But Solomon tagged along.

I hated this new fear burning inside me. I'd been afraid before. But it never lasted. Not like this. I knew I was supposed to trust God to take care of me. But all I could think of was the monster. And right now, it seemed a lot bigger than God.

The sun shone hot and wavy as we left Quentin's. "So what now?" I asked.

"Follow me," Dirt said. She took off running barefoot through the grass.

Solomon shrugged. Then we ran after her. Solomon kept up pretty well until we reached Dirt's special shortcut. She unhooked a thick vine from a tree by the gully. With two steps backward, she ran and leaped off the ground.

Clinging to the vine, Dirt swung across the gully and landed with a *whoop* on the other side.

I did the same, without the whoop. We waited for Solomon. He looked like a fish on the line, but he swung over. We grabbed his arms to help him the rest of the way up.

"Far out," Dirt told him. "Hope for you yet, Sol."

Dirt wound her way through the forest of trees. She stopped at the biggest maple tree and reached behind it. "Nobody says a word about my hiding place," she warned. Then she pulled out two fishing rods.

I still didn't know what Dirt had in mind. If Bingo Bob couldn't catch the monster, we sure couldn't. We were almost to the lake when something dropped from the tree above us. Solomon and I screamed and grabbed on to each other.

"Monster!" shouted Sam Benson, laughing.

"Funny, Sam," I said.

Dirt hadn't even slowed her stride. She kept going toward the lake.

"Where're you guys off to?" Sam asked.

"Dirt has a plan. *We're* trying to get rid of the monster," Solomon said, "which is more than I could say for some individuals."

"If you mean me and the Vultures," Sam said, "I can't get Ben or Marty to leave the clubhouse. They won't go near the lake since they saw the monster."

"Big, brave Vultures," I said, a little happy that I wasn't the only coward.

"Can I come?" Sam asked.

"I guess," I said, secretly glad to have somebody else along. "But you'll have to ask Dirt if you can stay."

Dirt was already waist-deep in the lake when we walked up. She told Sam he could stay as long as he did what he was told.

"Sam could take my place," I offered.

"No way," Dirt said. She handed her rod to Solomon and threw the second rod into the rowboat. Then she pulled the rowboat from shore and hopped in. "Here's the plan," Dirt said. "Sol will fish for it. Molly, you and Sam and I can dive for the monster."

6

Creature of the Deep

I tried everything I could think of to get out of Dirt's plan. There was no way I wanted to go swimming with some creature of the deep. But Dirt has a way of making me go along. And I found myself sitting in the silver rowboat, floating to meet the monster.

The rowboat rocked, and I screamed.

"Cool it," Dirt said. "You want to scare it away?"

Yes, I thought. That's exactly what I want.

Sam and I weren't rowing fast enough for Dirt. She jumped back into the water and began pulling the boat by the tie-up rope. I watched, fearing every minute something would swim up and eat Dirt.

Solomon picked up the fishing rod. The hook caught his shorts. He pulled the line, ripping his shorts. Then the fishing rod flew overboard.

"What a klutz!" Sam said, shaking his head.

We were almost to the center of the lake. My heart pounded.

"This is good," Dirt called from the water. "Molly and Sam, come on in. We'll dive to the bottom and look for the monster."

That was Dirt's plan? I couldn't do it. "Dirt," I said, "I can't go in. I-I-I didn't bring my swimsuit." It was a lie, and I felt bad the minute it was out. But I was so frightened, I wasn't thinking straight.

"It's under your shirt, Molly," Dirt said.

Sam stood up, rocking the boat again. "Geronimo!" cried Sam. Then he dived into the dark water.

I knew Sam wasn't all that brave. He'd do anything without thinking about it. That's all.

Sam burst through the water with a loud, monsterlike noise. "Last one in's a rotten egg," he yelled.

"I'm coming," I said. I took off my shirt and shorts and straightened my swimsuit. *Please, God,* I prayed, *don't let the monster get me.* I stuck my foot in the warm water, then eased myself off the side of the boat.

The water felt warm like the sun. I swam out toward Dirt but hit a cold spot. The lake turned freezer cold, sending shivers through my whole body. What if the monster lay in wait right there? What better place for it to live than a dank, cold spot like this one?

The slimy, moss reeds of my dreams brushed my legs like fingers. I turned and lunged back into the boat.

"What is it, Molly?" Dirt asked. I don't think she had any idea how scared I was.

"Nothing," I said, breathing heavily. "I just thought we'd do better if I got us some reeds to breathe through. I'll row over to the side and get some," I offered.

"Far out," Dirt said. She took a deep breath and duck-dived straight down, her toes kicking up out of the water. I watched her go down, but the murky lake covered her.

Sam treaded water. Solomon and I looked on from the boat. Dirt still didn't come up. Sam caught my eye and looked a little worried.

"Can you see her?" I asked.

He shook his head.

It seemed like another minute before we saw little bubbles rise to the surface of the lake. Then Dirt's head popped out of the water. She was grinning. She held up her hand. In it was an old baseball bat, soggy and rotten. "Cool!" she said. "I lost this a couple of summers ago." And down she went for more.

Solomon and I paddled slowly to the other shore. I kept looking back to make sure Sam and Dirt were okay.

"What are we getting?" Solomon asked. He struggled with his oar in the water. Our boat spun in a circle, then zagged toward shore again.

"A reed," I explained. "A hollow weed. They can breathe through one end and go deep, as long as the top of the reed stays out of the water." I said *they* because I wanted to make sure we only found two reeds. I wasn't going back into that lake.

The boat bumped the shore. I hopped out on land and pulled the boat up.

Solomon jumped out and ran toward the weeds. "You stay there, Molly," he called. "I'll get the reeds."

I wanted to get the reeds—two reeds. But Solomon had pulled three good ones and was back before I got the boat tied. Quentin was right. He *was* a pest.

We started back. "Oops," I said. I let one reed slip into the water. "Well, guess I don't need one." We paddled back to Dirt and Sam. "Sorry, guys," I said. "We only made it back with two reeds." I gave them each one.

Sam and Dirt plunged back down toward the lake bottom. I felt guilty watching them fade into the murk. First I'd let Quentin face the monster alone. Now Dirt and Sam. What was wrong with me anyway? It was like I couldn't hear any voice except fear.

Dirt kept coming back up with junk from the lake. Soggy balls, screwdrivers, a Thermos bottle.

"Haley's doll," she said, a minute later. She tossed me a smelly, plastic doll with seaweed clinging where hair should have been. "I threw this in the lake last year," Dirt said.

Sam surfaced, holding something between his teeth. The part out of the water looked like a yellow sponge, but smoother. He took it out of his teeth and held it up high. "Look what I found!" he said. "And it looks new too. I had to tug it hard to get it loose. I think the weeds had it wrapped up."

The thing was like a giant sponge snake, smooth and squishy, shaped like a long baseball bat.

"I think it's a water snake," I said. "Chuckie has one. He uses it to float. Mom calls it a water noodle."

"Well, it's mine now," Sam said. He threw it into the boat and jumped in after it.

"Come on, Dirt," I said. "Fish don't like the daylight. I don't think the Lake-Ness monster does either. We might as well go."

"Yes," Solomon said, "we should go."

Dirt didn't want to, but she nodded agreement and swam to shore.

Quentin was standing on shore when we pulled the boat in.

"Quentin," I called, "you came!"

"I had to get out of there before Granny Mae forced a second bowl of cereal on me."

"Peanut butter cereal?" Solomon asked, stepping to shore.

Quentin shot his cousin a hot glare. Then he looked like he might toss his cookies all over again. "Go home, Solomon," he said. "I'll handle this problem from here."

Solomon stomped off through the woods without looking back.

"Any monster sightings?" Quentin asked.

"We need night," Dirt said.

"I have been doing a bit of research on water phenomena," Quentin said. "There is a chance we may have happened onto the species of fish called the Siluris glanis. To the unscientific it is known as the giant catfish. This 400-pound fish lives in the rivers of Eastern Europe. It has been known to swallow ducks and geese whole."

I felt like *I* might toss *my* cookies. If the thing could swallow large ducks whole, why not small people? I moved farther away from the lake.

"Might I suggest a formal meeting of the Cinnamon Lake Mystery Club this evening? Would that be agreeable?" asked Quentin.

"Cool!" Dirt said. "Like eight. That'll give us time to trap the monster at the lake tonight."

I'd always loved being in the woods at night. Now the idea terrified me. The fear was growing inside like a disease, taking over. I tried to think of an excuse why I couldn't make the meeting.

A loud, grinding noise exploded from the lake. Nobody moved. A roar and a growl traveled across the water.

I think my heart stopped. I couldn't breathe.

Behind me I heard Dirt whisper. "We know you're there, Lake-Ness monster. Tonight we're going to get you!"

7

Lady Lake-Ness

I was a few minutes late to our Cinnamon Lake tree house that night. I'd brought Sam with me so I wouldn't have to walk through the woods alone. Dirt was hanging on her branch already. Quentin and Solomon sat on the far ends of Quentin's branch.

Sam climbed to Sunny's branch, and I kept climbing to mine.

"May I be so bold as to ask what Samuel is doing here?" Quentin asked, settling onto his tree branch.

"Sam did a good job hunting for the monster this afternoon," I said. "I thought he might be a help tonight." I also thought I might be able to work it out so Sam could take my place. I'd decided that no matter what, I wasn't going into that lake. Not ever.

"No fair," Haley said from below. She was the last to arrive as usual. "I told Dirt I didn't want anything to do with this monster. If she hadn't threatened to be a tattletale, I'd be home watching the Miss Teen America pageant right now."

Haley climbed to her branch, the lowest. "But no-o-o. Dirt would tell Mother I've been using her lipstick."

Dirt, hanging upside down by her knees like a monkey, gave the thumbs-up sign.

I called the meeting to order. "I was thinking," I began. "What if we just left the Cinnamon Lake-Ness monster right where it is? Wouldn't that be okay? Maybe it would get bored and go back to where it came from." I tried to act like it didn't make any difference to me.

An owl hooted, and I grabbed my branch so hard, my fingernails filled with bark.

"No way!" Sam said. "I say we get the big lug out of our lake!"

"Right on," Dirt said.

"Perhaps for the sake of science, we should solve this mystery," said Quentin. "As unlikely as it seems, I agree with Samuel."

We fell silent. I heard little gray cells buzzing. I was trying to think up a plan to get myself out of this. I figured the rest of them were trying to come up with a plan to get rid of the Lake-Ness monster.

"I believe I have come up with a workable plan," Solomon said, sounding just like Quentin.

"Go, Sol!" Dirt said.

"He can't have a plan," Haley whined. "He's not a member of the Cinnamon Lakers."

"He can have a plan, Haley," I said. "Go ahead, Solomon."

"Thank you, Molly," Solomon said. "Perhaps I'd best give a bit of history on the original Loch Ness monster. The monster had been sighted in Scotland for centuries when a group of English firemen devised a plan to better observe the monster. They invented their own monster, a lady monster, to lure the unsuspecting fellow from the depths of the lake."

"Solomon, you're a genius!" Sam said. "Quentin, you better look out. This guy's going to pass you up one day, if he hasn't already. Great idea, kid!"

Quentin folded his arms over his chest. "Harrumph," he muttered.

"More," Dirt demanded.

"We make our own monster," Solomon said. "A lady monster. Then we set her out on Cinnamon Lake and let the Cinnamon Lake-Ness monster come to us."

"Cool," Dirt said. "Lady Lake-Ness monster."

Frankly, I was hoping Solomon's idea would stink. But the plan sounded good to me. It might even work.

"How do you know the one in the lake is a male monster?" Quentin challenged.

"I did not claim the plan was foolproof," Solomon said.

"*Fool* is the correct word, if you ask my opinion," Quentin said.

"Who cares if it's a girl or a boy?" Sam said. "If it's a girl, she'll probably like to see another girl. Girl talk, you know? But I think it's a guy. He's so big."

"I don't know," I said. "How could we make a girl monster *if* we wanted to?"

"I could probably think of a simple structure," Solomon offered. "Does anyone have a raft in the shape of an animal?"

"You do, Molly," Sam said. "That horse one. The gray thing."

"That's Chuckie's raft," I said. I knew which one he meant. But Chuckie wasn't big on sharing.

"*I* could make it look like a woman," Haley said. "I can make it look beautiful. I know all kinds of beauty secrets."

"Deal," Dirt said, jumping to the ground.

"Let us meet back here in an hour," Solomon said. "Bring bright flashlights."

Quentin, Solomon, and I crossed the woods together since we live in the same direction. They weren't talking to each other. And I wasn't talking either. Not to anybody. I'd wanted to get myself out of this. Instead, I was on my way to make a monster.

Long shadows stretched across the woods, leaving bars on the ground, like a jail cell. *Lord,* I prayed, watching in every direction, in case the Lake-Ness monster decided to roam around on the land, *help me get out of this mess. I don't want to meet a monster.*

8

The Making of a Monster

Chuckie threw a fit when he caught me carrying his horsey raft out of the garage. The raft had a long body, like a regular float or air mattress. But in front was a horse head, with plastic reins.

"Chuckie swim!" he cried. He tackled my ankle.

"You should be asleep," I said.

"Chuckie ride Horsey!" he demanded.

"No, I'm just borrowing Horsey for a little while," I explained.

"Chuckie come!" he cried.

"Chuckie stay," I said.

"Chuckie come!" he cried again, still hanging on to my leg.

"Chuckie stay!" I pleaded.

Mom stuck her head in. "What's going on here?"

That was Chuckie's cue for tears. "Mowry take Chuckie's horsey!" He rubbed his eyes and wailed.

Mom raised her eyebrows at me.

"I'm just borrowing it, Mom," I said.

"It's awfully late, Molly," Mom said. "Do you really need the raft?"

"Yeah," I said. "I'm not going out alone. Quentin and Solomon, Haley, Dirt, and Sam are meeting me. They wanted the raft."

Then it hit me. Why was I trying so hard? If I couldn't take the raft, maybe the other Cinnamon Lakers would give up the plan. "But hey, Mom," I said quickly, "if you don't want me to take it …" I started to put the raft back.

"No," Mom said, "Chuckie and I need to have a little talk about sharing. You go on. But don't be late. Chuckie would love to share. Wouldn't you, Chuckie?"

"Chuckie no share!" he screamed.

Mom dragged my screaming brother inside the house.

The walk through the woods took me longer than usual. I kept hearing sticks break or animals call. When I got to the tree house, everybody was waiting for me.

" 'Bout time," Dirt said.

I handed over Horsey. "Take good care of him," I said. "Chuckie will kill me if anything happens to Horsey."

"Oooh," Haley cooed. "Put *her* right here. This is going to be so fun!" She set her flowered bag on the ground and took things out. "I'm going to make you beautiful," she told Horsey.

Dirt rolled her eyes.

Haley tied a scarf around Horsey's neck. She put Sam and Quentin to work gluing a wig to the horse head. I acted as her nurse, handing her the "instruments" as she called for them: "Rouge!" "Eyeliner!" "Powder!"

"What am I supposed to do?" Solomon asked, leaning over Quentin's shoulder.

"Stop breathing down my neck for one thing," Quentin said.

Solomon didn't answer, but he backed up.

"The real monster has 18 eyes," Sam said. "Give her lots of eyes."

"It does not," Dirt said. "It's slimy."

"I remember a huge head," I said.

We went back and forth on what the monster looked like. We couldn't agree on much, except that it was scary.

"Look at her," Haley said. "Isn't she just perfect? Now this." Haley took out two little strips of hair that looked like fringe.

"Mom's false eyelashes," Dirt said.

Haley glued them above Horsey's eyes. "Mother doesn't look as glamorous in them," Haley said.

"Aren't you done yet?" Sam asked.

"You can't hurry beauty," Haley said. She continued to work her magic on Horsey. Finally she drew out a tube of red lipstick and made huge, puffy lips on the horse.

I had to admit, Horsey did look like a girl— maybe even something a monster would find attractive. "Not bad, Haley," I admitted.

"Not bad?" Haley protested. "I'm a miracle worker. I might even be able to make Dirt look like a girl if she'd let me."

"Over my dead body," Dirt said.

"Let's name it ... *Haley*," Sam suggested.

"It does look like Haley," Quentin agreed.

"No-o-o!" Haley whined.

Sam scooped up the monster and set it on his shoulder. He whirled around. "Oh, fair Haley," Sam said dramatically, "you are so beautiful."

"Stop it!" Haley cried. "Don't call her that."

"*Haley, Haley*," Sam sang. He skipped down the hill to the lake, with the real Haley chasing after him.

Quentin and Solomon walked ahead of me. I lagged behind. I was in no hurry to get to Cinnamon Lake. Ahead of me, I heard Quentin and Solomon arguing.

"... stupidest idea I've ever heard of," Quentin was saying. "Entirely unscientific. I'm almost ashamed to call you my cousin."

"Yes, I know," Solomon said.

"I'd still like to know what you've done with certain items from my laboratory," Quentin said. "My weights? My pulleys? Honestly, Solomon, no wonder your parents wanted to get rid of you."

"They didn't," Solomon said. "I wanted to come."

"Well, nobody asked me if I wanted you to come," Quentin said.

Solomon stopped in his tracks. I almost ran into the back of him. It didn't feel right listening in on a family feud. So I ran to catch up with the others. But when I looked back over my shoulder, Solomon was running away into the woods.

It was dark back in the woods. But the sky brightened the lake. Above I could see Venus and parts of the Milky Way. The lake shimmered with sparkles of light. But none of it looked beautiful to me. Not like it always had before tonight.

Even the stars seemed to promise something horrible was about to happen.

Clouds rushed across the moon, making the light flash on and off.

"I forgot perfume," Haley said.

Sam plunked our monster on the bank next to the lake. "Monsters stink, Haley."

"Be careful with her," I said. "Chuckie will kill me if I hurt Horsey." Then I wished I'd picked a different word than *kill.* The real Cinnamon Lake-Ness monster was lurking out there on the dark lake. Waiting. Watching.

"Launch it," Sam said.

"Wait! Here, Haley," Dirt said, handing her something. "You forgot her hat."

"It's adorable!" Haley said. She put the bonnet on the lady monster's head and tied it under her chin. Haley stood back and admired the straw hat with little flowers. "I love this hat, Dirt. I have one just like it."

"Not anymore," Dirt said. And she launched Lady Lake-Ness into the angry waters of Cinnamon Lake.

9

Monster Attack!

I watched as Lady Lake-Ness floated across Cinnamon Lake. Her bonnet shone in the moonlight.

"Do your thing, dear," Haley called softly.

"Where's Sol?" Dirt asked.

Quentin looked toward the woods. "He ... uh ... thought of something he had to do at the house." He stretched his neck and peered into the dark woods. "I do hope he has the sense to go directly home. Solomon is not used to outdoor life."

"No sweat," Sam said. "That's one smart kid, Quentin. A real chip off the old block."

Quentin looked puzzled, then proud. "I suppose he is at that," he said. "Perhaps I should look for him."

"Shh-hhh!" Dirt scolded.

I didn't hear anything. But Dirt's ears hear a lot ours don't.

A cloud passed over the moon, and I had trouble making out the form of our monster. Then the moon cleared.

"Help!" Haley yelled. "Look! The monster has her!"

Lady Lake-Ness was spinning, turning in circles. Ripples and air bubbles foamed all around her. She spun faster and faster.

"He's got her now!" Sam yelled.

Lady Lake-Ness flopped first one way, then the other. Nothing in Cinnamon Lake we'd ever seen could make our monster act like that. It was as if some force had hold of her and was shaking her.

"We have to save her!" Haley screamed.

It was Chuckie's raft, but I didn't care. I wanted to be home. My heart pounded so loudly, every other sound faded. I felt like *I* was drowning, drowning in my own fears.

Suddenly, as if Lady Lake-Ness gave up, she collapsed. She folded in on herself and sank.

"He's killed her!" yelled Haley.

Dirt headed for the water, but Sam grabbed her arm. "Don't, Dirt," he said. "We don't know what's out there."

In the exact spot where Lady Lake-Ness had gone down, the water began to fizzle. It bubbled and rippled. Then up through the water rose a gigantic figure. The Cinnamon Lake-Ness monster!

Screams came from all sides of me. But not from me. I was frozen in terror. I couldn't open my mouth to scream.

"I see it!" yelled Quentin. "This is history! This is science in the making!"

Like a long, fat, ugly snake, its monstrous head bobbed from side to side, as if looking for more people to eat. Its round body sat on the surface of the lake, rocking back and forth. Moss, seaweed, sticks, and leaves covered the beast. It seemed to glide over the face of the water.

"Far out," Dirt said.

A yell came from the monster. A horrible scream.

"That sounded human," Sam said.

The cry came again. "Help! Help! Help me!"

It *was* human. I knew that voice. But I couldn't think clearly.

"Solomon!" Quentin cried.

In the light of the moon, we could see Solomon hanging onto the neck of the monster. He flopped just like Lady Lake-Ness had.

"My little cousin!" Quentin cried. "Solomon!"

I had to do something. *Father,* I prayed, *You're stronger than monsters. You're bigger than fear. Help me help Solomon.*

Without another thought, I kicked off my thongs and ran toward the water until I was swimming. Swimming toward the Cinnamon Lake-Ness monster. *Even though I swim in the valley of the shadow of death,* I told myself, not slowing my stroke, *I'll fear no evil.* I kept kicking the water, heading straight for Solomon.

Behind me, I heard splashing. Somebody was in the lake behind me. Beside me. In front of me. Passing me with lightning speed. Quentin! Quentin was swimming toward the Cinnamon Lake-Ness monster.

"Hold on, Solomon!" he yelled. I heard Quentin swallow lake water, gurgle, and yell again. "I'm coming, Cousin!"

All the while, Solomon had been hollering and bobbing about in the water. Suddenly his cries stopped.

From where I was, I saw Quentin, his arms waving wildly, jump at the monster. "Take that, you scoundrel! Leave my cousin alone!" Quentin leaped out of the water and landed on the back of the Cinnamon Lake-Ness monster!

10

Monstrous Love

I swam faster to reach the monster. Solomon was hollering again. But this time, he was yelling at Quentin. "Stop, Quentin! Stop!" he screamed.

Quentin splashed madly in the water. I couldn't even see him through the spray. "Unhand my cousin!" he cried. "I'll teach you to—" He stopped. Quentin had one hand around the monster's neck. He held still in the water and stared at the long, thin neck.

The monster's neck came off in his hand. It was only a water noodle, a long sponge like the one Sam had found that afternoon.

I swam beside Quentin. The neck of the monster had been tied to a huge black circle, covered with seaweed and sticks. Underneath, it was nothing but a truck inner tube.

That was our Cinnamon Lake-Ness monster.

Quentin held on to one side of the truck tube. On the other side, Solomon was hanging on. They stared at each other across the inner tube.

I grabbed onto the *monster.* Quentin and Solomon still locked stares. I was the first to speak. "Solomon," I said, "it was you all along? *You're* the Cinnamon Lake-Ness monster?"

Solomon looked down at the tube and nodded slowly.

"It can't be!" I said. "I saw the monster come out of the deep part of the lake."

"I stored it there," he explained. "I used Quentin's air compressor and ran a tube into the reeds. When I let the air out, the monster sank to the bottom with weights. When I blew it up from the reeds, where I hid the compressor, it rose to the surface. Simple physics, really."

"That's why you didn't want *me* to go into the reeds and get some for the swim search this afternoon," I said. It was starting to come together now. It explained the water noodle Sam found too. And Quentin's missing air compressor and weights.

"But why? Why did you do it, Solomon?" I asked.

"To prove to all of you I could," he said. "You thought I was only a little kid who could not fit in with your group. The Lake-Ness monster was a joke." But he didn't sound like even he thought it was funny.

"Is everybody okay?" Sam called from the bank. Haley hid behind him.

I waved to them. "We're okay!" I yelled to shore.

Dirt popped up out of the water through the center of the inner tube. She turned from Solomon to Quentin. Then without a word, she popped down under the water and swam away.

"You shouldn't have called for help," I said. "We really thought you were in trouble, Solomon."

"I'm sorry," Solomon said. "I never thought any of you would try to come in after me. You don't even like having me around." He turned to Quentin, who still hadn't said a word. "Especially you, Quentin. I can't believe you swam out here just to save me."

"Did you say *just*?" Quentin said. "Just to save my favorite cousin? No, of course you wouldn't think I'd try to save you."

"Did you say favorite cousin?" Solomon asked.

Quentin went on as if he hadn't heard the question. "You do not know the first thing about saving people, Solomon."

Quentin let go of the tube and swam toward shore. Solomon and I swam after him. The air felt cool when I stepped out of the lake. Dirt was already there with Sam and Haley.

"Look what we found!" Haley said. She held out a tape recorder.

Sam reached over and pressed the play button on the tape player. A huge roar came from the speaker. The *monster's* roar.

"I'm really sorry," Solomon said to all of us. Then he turned to Quentin. "Quentin," he said, "you actually thought there was a monster in the lake, but you jumped in anyway. I don't get it. It's like you were willing to die to save me."

Quentin didn't answer.

I felt a calm and peace that I hadn't felt since Haley first saw the Cinnamon Lake-Ness monster. And my peace wasn't because there wasn't really a monster. It was because Jesus had given me courage when I needed it most.

"Solomon," I said, "you're right. Saving somebody isn't easy to understand. It does seem stupid to save somebody when it might cost you your own life."

Quentin turned and frowned at me.

"I wasn't saying you're stupid, Quentin." I tried again. "I just meant that saving is what Jesus did first. He gave up His life so we could have ours. That's what saving is. And that's kind of why Quentin came in to save you."

Dirt slapped Solomon on the back. He almost fell over. "We're fishers of men, Solly," she said.

Quentin grinned and scruffed his cousin's head. "Even if those men *are* little monsters," he said.

It was a great walk home. Quentin had his arm around his cousin. Sam broke off to go to his house on the other side of the lake. Then Haley and Dirt split off toward their house. Quentin and Solomon walked with me until we got to my street.

"If you like, we can walk you all the way home, Molly," Quentin said. "It is quite late."

"No thanks, Quentin," I said. "I'm not afraid."

11

One Last Monstrous Show

The next morning, we met at the lake for a search. Not a monster search this time. A search for what was left of Lady Lake-Ness. I wanted to get Chuckie's raft back for him.

"It shouldn't be too far from where we were last night," Solomon said. "I just let the air out of it. It sank pretty fast—with some fine circles as I recall."

We all recalled. It didn't take long to find both "monsters" and pull them to shore. Chuckie's was in pretty good shape.

"I've still got one question for you, Solomon," I said. "How'd you manage to get those big bones in the lake? You were with me every minute."

"That was not part of my construction," Solomon said. "I did not touch bones."

"Then who did?" I asked.

"You mean the bones on Bingo Bob's line?" Sam asked. "That was Ben and Marty. They did some bragging on that one. Said you guys looked like little babies. They stuck them on Bingo Bob's line when he was yelling at you and Solomon."

Ben and Marty! Those guys burned me up. They were the real Cinnamon Lake monsters.

That gave me an idea. A great idea. "Just a minute," I said, as Sam and Quentin folded the truck inner tube. "I'm getting an idea. A monstrous idea, in fact. What do you say we arrange one more visit from Mr. and Mrs. Lake-Ness monster?"

"Cool!" Dirt said.

Quentin and Solomon shook hands. Then they each grabbed a monster and started to work. Sam helped with Mr., and Haley helped with Mrs. Lake-Ness. Dirt and I worked out exactly how to give Ben and Marty the scare of their lives.

It took all day. But when we finished, both monsters looked better—that is, worse—than ever.

"Look who's coming!" Dirt said.

Over the far hill, just in front of the setting sun, two figures made their way toward the lake. One was tall and skinny, the other short and round. Marty and Ben. Both had fishing poles slung over their shoulders.

"Hide, everybody!" I said.

Solomon took his place in the reeds by the air compressor.

"The show's about to begin," I whispered.

"What show?" Haley asked.

"It's a show you won't want to miss," I said. "The Cinnamon Lake-Ness monsters meet the Vultures."

Help the Cinnamon Lakers solve these mysteries too!

56-1812

56-1813

56-1832

56-1833

12-3334

56-3362